DUDES,

THE SCHOOL IS HAUNTED!

D0299643

3302406061

Look for these
ROTTEN SCHOOL
books, too!

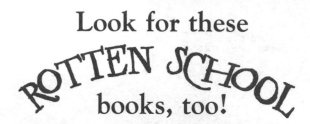

The Big
Blueberry
Barf~Off!

The Great
Smelling Bee

The Good,
the Bad and
the Very Slimy

Lose, Team,
Lose!

Shake, Rattle,
& Hurl!

The Heinie
Prize

ROTTEN SCHOOL

GROWTH · LEARNING · PIZZA!

DUDES, THE SCHOOL IS HAUNTED!

R.L. STINE

Illustrations by Trip Park

 HarperCollins*Publishers*
A Parachute Press Book

For Dad
–TP

First published in the USA by HarperCollins *Children's Books* 2006
First published in the UK by HarperCollins *Children's Books* 2007
HarperCollins *Children's Books* is an imprint of HarperCollins*Publishers* Ltd,
77-85 Fulham Palace Road, Hammersmith London W6 8JB

The HarperCollins *Children's Books* website address is
www.harpercollinschildrensbooks.co.uk

1 3 5 7 9 8 6 4 2

Dudes, The School is Haunted!
Copyright © 2006 by Parachute Publishing, L.L.C.
Cover copyright © 2006 by Parachute Publishing, L.L.C.

ISBN-10 0-00-721623-8
ISBN-13 978-0-00-721623-9

Printed and bound in England by
Clays Ltd, St Ives plc

GROWTH LEARNING PIZZA!

—:CONTENTS:—

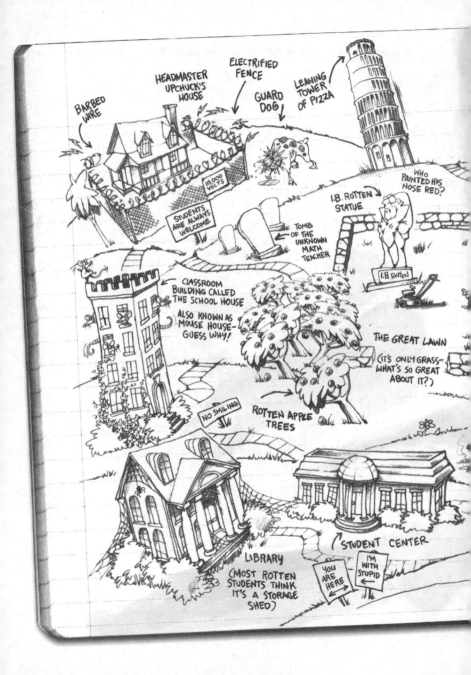

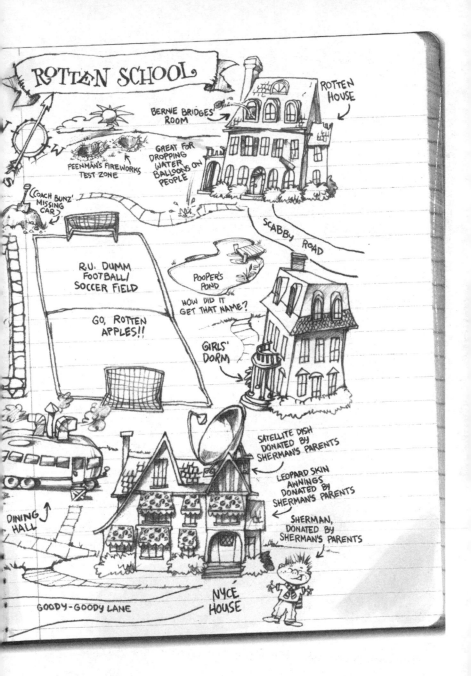

Good morning, Rotten Students. This is Headmaster Upchuck with today's Morning Announcements. I hope you will stop hitting one another until the announcements are over. Thank you and have a Rotten Day!

Chef Baloney announces that he will no longer be serving alphabet cereal for breakfast because of the disgusting words some of you have been leaving in your bowls.

A special treat in the Dining Hall tonight. Chef Baloney promises that the chickens will be plucked before they are served.

Nurse Hanley would like to remind all students who come down with stomach flu – you DO need a signed permission slip if you wish to vomit. The slips are available every morning from six to seven.

Third grader Harry Chest announces that the two thousand poisonous spiders in his collection escaped during the night. If you are bitten by one of these deadly spiders, DO NOT panic. We have sent away for a cure, which should be here in two to three weeks.

Attention, students who wish to play a musical instrument. Our music teacher, Mr Buzz Off, will be giving Air Guitar lessons after school. You do not have to bring your own instrument. Mr Buzz Off says he will bring enough air guitars for everyone.

And finally, for all students who are interested in science, second grader Billy Gote will be showing off the oozing green and purple scabs on his knees at dinner tonight.

Chapter 1

THE GHOST WALKS AT NIGHT!

Warning: if you're afraid of ghosts, you'd better stop here.

Because, dudes, Rotten School is *haunted*!

I should know. *I'm* the one who is haunting it.

You've probably heard of me. I'm Bernie Bridges, fourth-grade superstar. I don't like to brag. But *how else* can I describe myself?

Catch these dimples when I smile. *Killer* – right?

If you've heard of me, you've probably heard of Joe Sweety, too. Sweety is the biggest, meanest, fiercest, bulliest, smackdown kid at Rotten School.

If he bites you, you *definitely* get rabies. No joke.

We call him The Big Sweety. He works out *thirty* hours a day. Really. Joe can bruise you with his *hair*!

He's *huge*! He even has muscles on his *teeth*! The fronts of his T-shirts all say EXTRA-WIDE LOAD.

Get the picture? Sweety is *not* a sweetie.

So, what does this have to do with the school being haunted? Who set the evil ghost loose? And why has it chosen Joe Sweety as its next victim? Well, don't get your boxers in a knot. You'll find out soon. I can't tell you *everything* in the first chapter – *can* I?

Let's start at the beginning. Our field trip to the zoo...

Chapter 2

AWK! AWK!

"Awk! Awk!"

"Uhk~uhk~uhk!"

"Mweek~mweek~mweeek!"

Those are my friends, Feenman and Crench, making bird sounds. Ha-ha. They're a riot. Now they're bending over, flapping their arms and marching around like storks.

"AWK! AWK!"
"GULLLLLP!"

Oops. Feenman just swallowed his gum.

These two guys are my best buddies because they like to have fun. Feenman can make forty-two different disgusting noises by cracking his knuckles. And Crench collects dead flies. He has a drawer full of them.

Fun dudes, right?

Why are they imitating birds today? Well, I told you – this is where our ghost story starts. In the Bird House at the Lousy Town Zoo.

Mr I B Rotten is the man who opened the Rotten School a hundred years ago. He had a rich friend named Louie B Lousy. And Louie B Lousy built the zoo.

The Lousy Town Zoo is small and not too thrilling. I mean, they have a three-legged elephant. How sad is that?

Feenman, Crench and I went into the Panda House. At first we thought the pandas were sleeping.

Then we realised they were all *stuffed*!

"Dudes, let's check out the Bird House," I said. "It's gotta be more interesting than this!"

BIRDS FROM AROUND THE WORLD.

That's what the sign said. But the first cage had a turkey in it. And the second cage had a sick little yellow canary clinging to its perch.

Our friend Beast stood staring into the canary cage. He kept shoving white fluffy stuff into his mouth.

"Beast, where'd you get the popcorn?" Crench asked.

"It's not popcorn," he said. "I got it off the bottom of that birdcage." He held out a handful. "Want some?"

"*Ulllp*… no thanks," Crench said. "Why don't I just go throw up in the corner over there?"

Feenman let out a groan. "What stinks? Oh, wow. I just stepped in something really gross." He started scraping the bottom of his shoe against a birdcage.

I slapped my buddies on the back. "Are we having an *awesome* time or what?"

You probably think we *hated* the Lousy Town Zoo. But you're wrong.

We all loved it when our teacher, Mrs Heinie, took the whole fourth grade on a field trip into town. No classes! No schoolwork!

Going into town is a big deal for us. You see, the Rotten School is a boarding school. We live at school. We can't get out unless someone lets us out.

So we were having an *excellent* time at the zoo. And we all groaned when Mrs Heinie poked her head into the Bird House and shouted it was time to leave.

I turned to Beast. "Hey, where's that canary?"

He grinned at me. He had feathers stuck in his teeth.

Beast loves field trips too.

But we had to leave. We lined up and started walking two by two to the yellow school bus. I moved next to my friend Chipmunk. He walked with his eyes down on the sidewalk.

Chipmunk is the shiest, most timid kid in school. He's so shy, he never looks up. He stares at his shoes all day.

"What's up, Chipper?" I asked. "How'd you like the zoo?"

He shivered. "A squirrel really scared me, Bernie."

"Huh?" I stared at him. "You were afraid of a squirrel?"

He lowered his head. "Well, it kinda sneaked up on me."

He pulled a red-and-yellow juice box from his backpack. He shoved in the straw and began sucking on it frantically.

"Thirsty?" I asked.

He shook his head. "It's apple juice. Sometimes it helps me. I get carsick. Real bad."

I shoved the straw back in his mouth. "Keep drinking!" I said. "And don't sit next to me!"

"MOVE IT!" a voice boomed behind us. Joe Sweety's voice. "OUT OF MY WAY!" Joe Sweety yelled.

"AWK! AWK! AWK!"

Those were *not* bird cries. Those were the squawks of a kid who didn't get out of The Big Sweety's way fast enough. Sweety stepped on him and walked right over him.

And now he clumped up behind Chipmunk and me.

"Yo, Big Sweety!" I said. "Lookin' good. You punch out any post boxes lately?"

On our last trip to town, a port boxes got into Sweety's way. He decided to fight it.

The mailbox lost.

"MOVE IT!" Sweety boomed again.

"Yikes!" Chipmunk got so scared, he squeezed his juice box. *And squirted apple juice into The Big Sweety's face!*

And believe it or not, that's where our ghost story started.

Here come some SCREAMS. Stick with me, dudes. Now it starts to get way SCARY.

Chapter 3

SCREAMS OF TERROR

"Oh, nooooooo!"

Kids screamed and shrieked and gasped.

Apple juice dripped down Sweety's beefy red face. His eyes were shut tightly. He gritted his teeth angrily.

Bernie B to the rescue. I always protect my guys.

"You wouldn't hurt my friend Chipmunk, would you?" I said. "He was only trying to cool you off. You know. Give you a little refreshment."

The Big Sweety
picked me up by the
ears. Then he set me
down on top of a car.

Then he moved
in on Chipmunk.

Chipmunk
started to shake
and quake.
"B-b-b-b—"
His lips moved up
and down, but no
words came out.
His eyes bulged out
of his head.

He was so
terrified, he
squeezed the juice box – *and squirted The Big Sweety
in the face AGAIN!*

The juice dripped down Sweety's face. He
uttered a deep growl.

Kids screamed and gasped.

Sweety turned. He grabbed Feenman's shirt –

and ripped it off Feenman's body. Then he mopped his face with it.

"H-help! H-help!" Chipmunk wailed. He dropped to his knees.

The Big Sweety took two giant steps toward Chipmunk. He raised his meaty fists.

I knew I had to act fast.

I did the only thing I could do.

I hid my eyes.

"I can't watch," I murmured. "I can't watch this."

Chapter 4

THE FIST BROTHERS

I held my breath and listened. But I didn't hear Chipmunk screaming in pain.

I peeked out between my fingers.

I saw Sweety pull Chipmunk gently to his feet. Then Sweety put a heavy arm around Chipmunk's trembling shoulders.

"Hey, no problem, dude," Sweety said, grinning at Chipmunk. "Accidents happen, right?" He pinched Chipmunk's cheek. "Right, buddy?"

My mouth dropped open. Was The Big Sweety *sick* or something?

Or was he just getting ready to clamp Chipmunk in a headlock and use his face to make mashed potatoes?

Sweety patted Chipmunk on the back. "That's my good buddy, the Chipper!" he said.

Then I realised what was up. Mrs Heinie was standing right there.

"Hi, Mrs Heinie," I said. "Good to see you!"

She had a stern scowl on her face. She had her hands at her waist and was leaning forward, squinting at Sweety through her thick glasses.

"What's up, Buster?" she asked Joe.

Sweety grinned at Mrs Heinie. "Just kidding around with my good buddy," he said. "We're sharing some apple juice."

Mrs Heinie squinted through her glasses. "You weren't going to hurt him – were you?"

"No way," Sweety replied. "That's my pal, the Chipper!" He grabbed Chipmunk's school tie and dragged him towards the bus. "You're sitting next to me, Chipper."

I let out a long breath. Thanks to Mrs Heinie, Chipmunk was still alive – at least for now.

I climbed on to the bus and started down the aisle, searching for a seat. Whoa! The seat next to April-May June was empty!

April-May is the hottest, coolest girl in Rotten School. She is my girlfriend. Only she doesn't know it yet. Actually she doesn't have a clue. She thinks I'm belly-button lint.

"Can I sit down?" I asked.

She narrowed her blue eyes at me. "You're joking, right?"

"Is the seat taken?" I asked.

"It will be," she said. "By someone else."

"I understand," I said, flashing her my smile with the adorable dimples. "You *want* me to sit next to you. But you're just *too shy* to ask me."

She tossed her head back and laughed.

I took a deep breath. Since she was in such a good mood, I decided to ask her my

big question. "April-May, next Saturday is movie night. They're showing a scary ghost movie at the Student Centre," I said. "Would

you like to go with me?"

She stuck a finger down her throat and made a gagging sound. Then she spat her bubblegum on to the pocket of my school blazer.

"Was that a yes or a no?" I asked.
Before she could answer, two strong hands

wrapped around my waist – and pulled me into the seat across from Chipmunk and Joe Sweety.

"You'll be going to the scary movie with *me*, Honey Cakes," a voice cooed.
Jennifer Ecch!
I call her Nightmare Girl. The Ecch is

almost as big and tough as Joe Sweety. *AND she's totally in love with me!*

Do you know how *embarrassing* it is to be in fourth grade and have a girl totally in love with you?

Yuck. She grabbed my hand, rolled up my sleeve and started planting loud, smoochy kisses up and down my arm.

"Stop! Stop it!" I cried. "You're sucking

off all my arm hair!"

The bus started to move. "Buckle up,

everyone!" Mrs Heinie called.

I was trapped. Trapped next to Jennifer Ecch.

The bus bumped down the street. The Ecch kept planting smoochy kisses up and down my arm.

Behind me, some kids started to sing

chorus after chorus of The Official Rotten School Song.

"Rah rah Rotten School!
I'd rather be in Rotten School
Than NOT in school!"

Beast stuck his head out the window and howled like a dog.

In front of me, Joe Sweety looked round to see if Mrs Heinie was watching. Then he raised a fist to Chipmunk. "Have you met Mr Fist?" he asked.

"N-n-n-no!" Chipmunk stuttered.
"Did you know that Mr Fist has a brother?" Sweety growled.

Chipmunk made a gulping sound. "N-no. What's *he* called?"
"Mr OTHER Fist," Sweety replied.
Chipmunk gulped again. I could see him

shaking and quaking in terror. "Th-that apple juice thing," Chipmunk stammered. "It was a total accident."

Sweety leaned closer to Chipmunk. "I hope you don't have an accident and run into Mr Fist!"

Suddenly, Mrs Heinie appeared in the bus aisle. "What are you up to, Buster?" she asked Joe Sweety.

Sweety lowered his fists. "Chipmunk and I were just talking about how much fun we

had at the zoo," Sweety said. "We *loved* the pandas – *didn't* we, Chipper? They were *awesome*."

"Actually," Chipmunk said, "I... I wish I'd stayed in the dorm, working on my hobby."

"What's your hobby?" Sweety asked him.

"Hiding under the bed."

Mrs Heinie walked back to her seat. The bus hit a hard bump.

"Ohhhhh! I feel WAY carsick!" Chipmunk moaned.

And then his mouth flew open and—

"ULLLLLLLLLLLLLLLLLLP!"

He *ullllllllll*ped all over Joe Sweety.

Chapter 5
CHIPMUNK'S LAST WORDS

The Big Sweety let out a huge roar. Then he ripped off Chipmunk's shirt and

used it to mop the puke off his own clothes.

"B-b-b-b—" Chipmunk was shaking

and quaking, making that sound again
with his lips.

With another loud roar, Sweety raised
Mr Fist to Chipmunk. "Any last words?" he
demanded.

Chipmunk gulped. "Uh … yeah," he muttered.

"Here are my last words… HELLLLLLLLP!" Mrs Heinie jumped into the aisle. She leaned over Joe Sweety. "Is there a problem here, Buster?"

"No way!" Sweety replied. "What could be the problem? I was just helping my buddy Chipper with his carsickness trouble."

"Very nice," Mrs Heinie said. She headed back to her seat.

Sweety turned back to Chipmunk. "You're gonna have fun at your playdate," he said. Chipmunk stared at him. "Playdate?"

Sweety nodded. "Yeah. With Mr Fist and Mr OTHER Fist."

Thunder boomed. The bus shook. I saw a jagged bolt of lightning hit the ground outside. Rain poured down, drumming hard on the bus roof.

Jennifer Ecch grabbed me. She squeezed my arms until they looked like drinking straws. "Are you scared of storms?" she asked.

Thunder boomed again. "I'm more scared of *you!*" I said. "Let *go* of me. You're leaving fingerprints all over my skin!"

She giggled. "You DO like to tease a girl!"

Lightning flashed.
The rain pounded down.

Sweety was still showing his fists to Chipmunk.
Was it a *tense* ride back to school?

Are goldfish made out of fish?
Finally, the bus squealed to a stop in front of the Student Centre. The door opened and we all pushed our way out into the rain.

WHERE AM I GOING?

Ducking our heads, we ran into the front hall.

We were all laughing and shivering and shaking off water. I heard a crashing boom of thunder…

…And all the lights went out.
Silence.
A few kids giggled.
I couldn't see a thing. There are no

windows in the front hall of the Student Centre.

No one moved. No one made a sound. And then I heard a scream. A high, endless scream of horror.

Chipmunk!

Chapter 6

DE-TROUSERED

The ceiling lights flickered back to life. A dim orange at first, then bright yellow.

My heart pounding, I turned. I couldn't bear to see what Sweety had done to my friend. Had he split him in two? From now on would he be Chip and Munk?

Whoa—!

I blinked. I blinked again. I didn't believe my eyes!

Joe Sweety stood there – in front of the whole class – with his trousers down around his ankles. He was wearing boxers with *yellow flowers* on them!

Kids started to laugh. Some kids screamed in shock.

"He's been DE-TROUSERED!!"

"I'm sorry!" Chipmunk wailed again. "It was an *accident*! Really! You gotta believe me!"

Sweety scowled angrily at him. He shook the two Fist Brothers in Chipmunk's face.

"It was an *accident*!" Chipmunk wailed. "When the lights went out, I…grabbed the nearest thing. I didn't mean to grab your trousers!"

Kids roared with laughter. Sweety turned beet red.

Mrs Heinie hurried over. Rainwater dripped off her glasses. "What's going on here, Buster?" she cried, staring at Joe Sweety. "Why are your trousers down around your ankles?"

"Well, I—"

She didn't give The Big Sweety a chance to talk. "Showing off your underpants to the whole school?" she cried. "Maybe you'd like to show them off to Headmaster Upchuck!"

"But— but— but—" Sweety started to sputter.

"Maybe Headmaster Upchuck will give you some pointers on how to keep your trousers on when you're

in school! Come with me!" And she dragged Joe Sweety out by one ear.

At the front door, Sweety turned and waved Mr Fist and Mr OTHER Fist at Chipmunk. "Don't forget your playdate!" he shouted.

Then he and Mrs Heinie disappeared out into the rain.

Chipmunk turned to me. His whole body shook. His teeth chattered. "Oh, wow," he murmured. "I'm doomed now, Bernie. Doomed!"

I put a hand under his chin and raised his head high. "Are you kidding?" I said. "You're a hero!"

His eyes bulged. "Huh?"

"Check this out," I said. "You squirted The Big Sweety in the face with apple juice. Twice! Then you *urrp*ed your breakfast all over him. Then you detrousered him in front of the whole fourth grade!"

I slapped Chipmunk on the back. "AND... you got away with it!" I cried. "Dude, you got away with it!"

Chipmunk gulped hard. His arms and legs shook like a scarecrow in the wind. "Did I?" he whispered.

── Chapter 7 ──

PARTY ON, DUDES!

Chipmunk was a true hero. The dude made a fool of The Big Sweety. We had to celebrate and go nuts. I invited all the guys in Rotten House to a party the next night in the Commons Room. (That's like our living room.)

How could we have a wild party with our dorm mother, Mrs Heinie, snooping around?

Well, Mrs Heinie joined a new club. Friday night is her Tattoo Club night. She and a bunch of other ladies drive to the tattoo parlor in town every Friday night and watch people get tattoos.

So the coast was clear. Rotten House dorm was all OURS! That meant we could *par-tee!*

Does Bernie B know how to throw a party? Does a penguin eat the yellow snow?

Nothing but the best for my buddy Chipmunk. We had *five* different kinds of pizza, including Chipmunk's favourite – no sauce, no cheese, just crust.

We had piles of doughnuts and bags and bags of lemon garlic tortilla chips. You know – health food. And we had dozens of our favorite candy – Nutty Nutty Bars, which I sold to the guys at a special price of two dollars each.

The dudes were all chugging can after can of Foamy Root Beer. You know their slogan: "It's So Foamy, It Stays on Your Face for Hours." We drink *gallons* of it every day – *and* we use it for shampoo.

I'd hung up some crepe paper streamers for decoration. But they didn't last long. Beast was shoving them into his mouth and sucking them down like spaghetti.

Then he jammed an entire pizza into his mouth and ate it. I don't know how he did it, but he had *tomato sauce* pouring out of his *nose!* Cool, huh?

Some girls wandered into the party. I saw April-May June and her friend Sharonda Davis. Flora and Fauna, the Peevish twins, were arguing over which kind of pizza to have.

But— whoa. Wait. Hold on a minute.

"Hey, guys, where's Chipmunk?" I called.

The room grew silent.

"We can't have the party without Chipmunk," I said. "Chipmunk is the MAN!"

I dragged Feenman and Crench away from the food table. "Go find him," I said. "He's probably hiding under his bed. Drag him down here. It's *his* party!"

But before they could move, we saw a boy stagger into the room. Chipmunk!

I took one look at him – and let out a scream! Kids gasped and cried out in shock. Beast coughed up a red streamer.

Something was different about Chipmunk. I stared at him. What *was* it?

And then I saw. His nose – it was *upside down*! With the nostrils facing UP!

Chapter 8

SWEETY'S REVENGE

Chipmunk staggered over to me. "Help me, Big B," he said in a whisper. "Help me. Please – turn my nose back the right way. I can't go out in the rain like this."

"Hold still," I said. "Grit your teeth. This is gonna hurt a little."

I grabbed his nose. It made a crackling sound as I spun it back into place.

He let out a moan, and his knees buckled. Feenman and Crench helped him to a chair.

"Chipmunk, who did this to you?" I asked.

Chipmunk groaned. "I met Mr Fist and Mr

OTHER Fist," he said. "And then I met Mr Turn Your Nose Upside Down."

I turned to my friends. "Joe Sweety can't get away with this!" I shouted. "He can't twist noses upside down any time he pleases!"

"Of *course* he can." Chipmunk moaned. "He said this was just a love tap. Sweety said when he's finished with me, I'm gonna flop around on the floor like a seal, go

and people will toss fish at me."

Beast laughed. "Hey, Seal Boy!" he called. "Seal Boy! Urk-urk-urk!" Beast honked like a seal.

The dude has a weird sense of humor.

I turned back to Chipmunk. He was trembling so hard, his chair was doing a tap dance on the floor.

"Forget about The Big Sweety," I said. "Check it out. This party is for YOU! You're the hero, dude! How about some pizza with just the crust?"

Chipmunk shook his head sadly. "No thanks,

Bernie. I have to go hide under my bed till school is over in June."

The poor guy was terrified. He stumbled out of the room holding his nose.

Crench turned to me. "Bernie, what are you going to do?"

I shook my fist. "Wait till I get my hands on Joe Sweety," I said. "I'll turn his *whole face* upside down. He'll be eating with his eyebrows!"

Feenman and Crench stared at me. "You're kidding, Bernie. You're going to *fight* him?"

I shook my head. "Of course not. I'm a talker, not a fighter. That's how we'll get Sweety. We'll use our brains."

"Huh?" Crench said. "Fight with our brains? Won't that *hurt?*"

I made a fist and tapped Crench on the forehead. "Knock-knock," I said.

"Who's there?" Crench replied.

"*No one!*" I said. "Leave the thinking to me, Crench. Save your brain. You need it for walking and chewing gum at the same time."

"Yeah," Crench said. "That's kinda hard."

Chapter 9

SCARY GHOST STORY III

I stayed up all night, thinking hard about Joe Sweety. But I didn't dream up a good plan for revenge. The great Bernie B was stumped.

Just before dinner the next day, I ran into April-May June on the Great Lawn. I knew she wanted to be my girlfriend. She was just too shy to show it.

"Beat it, Bernie," she said.

"There you go again," I said. "Pretending you're not *thrilled* to see me! Can I talk to you?"

She rolled her eyes. "Sorry. I'm busy."

"Busy? What are you doing?" I asked.

"Breathing," she said.

I laughed. Of *course* my girlfriend has an *awesome* sense of humour!

"Did you think about Saturday night?" I asked. "You know. The scary movie? It's called *Scary Ghost Story Three*. Want to come with me?"

"I'm busy Saturday night," she said. "I found a power drill in the wood shop, and I'm going to drill another eye socket into my head."

I stared at her. "Is that a no?"

Poor April-May. Just too shy to admit she likes me.

I thought about her all the way back to Rotten House.

I found Feenman and Crench up in their room. They were tying one another's school neckties. That's how they get dressed for dinner. They don't know how to tie their own ties. They only know how to tie one another's!

"Too bad you cowards missed it. I really did a number on The Big Sweety today!" I bragged. I swung a fist in front of me. "Now he knows better than to mess with Rotten House dudes. He won't be coming after Chipmunk any more."

I laughed. "You shoulda seen the look on his face. After I got done with Sweety, he was shaking like Jell-O in an earthquake!"

Feenman frowned at me. "You're lying, right?"

"You are *so* lying," Crench said.

"Yes, I'm lying," I said. "But a dude can daydream – can't he?" I sighed. "I still don't have a plan."

"You'll think of something, Big B," Feenman said.

"You tied the knot too tight!" Crench gasped. "I… can't… *breathe!*"

Their ties were totally knotted together. They were going to be late for dinner again.

I hurried down to Chipmunk's room to see how he was doing. "Hey, Chipper – what's up?" I called.

I stared into an empty room.

"Hey… Chipper? Chip-Chipmunk?" I shouted, glancing around. "You da man, Chipmunk. You da man! Where are you?"

I heard a soft chirp above my head. I looked up and saw him. Chipmunk was on the ceiling. He

had squeezed himself
into the ceiling light.

"What are you doing
up there?" I called.

He shrugged. "Just
hanging."

"I'll get a ladder," I
said. "Bernie B to the
rescue. I'll pull you
down."

He shook his head.
"No thanks. I'm fine
here. Really. I've got
water and everything."

I stared up at him. "You're *serious*? You want to *stay* up there? For how long?"

"Just till the end of the school year. It's safer. Really," Chipmunk said. "Mr Fist and Mr OTHER Fist can't reach me up here."

"But Chipmunk—" I started.

"Please go away," he begged. "I LIKE it up here!"

"OK, OK," I muttered.

"But, Bernie, could you bring a few sandwiches back from the Dining Hall and toss them up to me?"

"No problem," I said.

"No tuna salad, OK? The little bits of celery make me gag."

"No problem," I said again. "But I'm going to find a way to protect you, Chipmunk. I'm going to find a way to scare the pants off Joe Sweety so he'll never bother you again."

And wouldn't you know it? I found the answer the very next night at the movie…

Chapter 10

A-HAUNTING WE WILL GO

When I arrived, the auditorium at the Student Centre was packed with kids. The lights were already dimming. Headmaster Upchuck was waving frantically for everyone to take a seat.

Feenman and Crench were supposed to save me a seat in the front row. I was halfway down the aisle – when two powerful hands grabbed me around the waist.

Jennifer Ecch pulled me on to her lap and put her arm around my shoulder to keep me from escaping. "Bernie, will you protect me from the ghost?" she asked in a tiny voice.

"Unnnh… unnnnh… mmmunnnh," I replied. She was squeezing a little too hard.

I know I'm adorable. But this was *way* too embarrassing!

The lights went out. Kids started to settle down. From the back row, Beast burped really loud.

"It's the GHOST!" a boy shouted.

Wild laughter broke out. Several other guys burped.

"Quiet, everyone! I won't start the movie until everyone is quiet!" Headmaster Upchuck shouted.

Beast let go with another deep, juicy burp. This one lasted at least two or three minutes.

Finally, the movie started. Jennifer squeezed me tighter. The movie title floated on to the screen in ghostly white letters: SCARY GHOST STORY III.

"*Scary Ghost Story Two* is my favorite," Jennifer whispered. She nibbled on one of my ears.

"Mmunnnnh-unnnnh!" I cried. She wouldn't let go. I was *helpless*! I knew both ears could be *gone* before the movie ended!

I leaned forward and stared at the screen. A group of teenagers with backpacks were walking in the woods at night. The forest was silent except for the crunch of their footsteps.

"Let's set up camp," one of the boys said. "We'll be totally safe here in the woods with no one around."

They pulled out plastic tents and started to erect them.

Creepy music started. Something moved behind a tree. The camera turned and moved closer.

Slowly…slowly…a pale figure came into view.

The creature smiled and we could see his rotting teeth. His nose was gone – just a hole in his face. And his eye sockets were deep and dark and empty.

The evil ghost!

"Terrible, cheap special effects," Jennifer muttered. "It's just a man in a costume. *No way* that's as good as *Scary Ghost Story Two*."

The ghost floated towards the teenagers, raising its bony hands to attack them. The creepy music grew louder.

I heard a scream – a high, shrill scream of horror.

At first I thought it was part of the movie. But then, down at the end of my row, I saw a kid jump up.

The kid let out another frightened scream, like a baby's cry. He pushed his way into the aisle and ran towards the door at the back, shrieking and wailing the whole way.

I turned to watch. *Chipmunk?* Was Chipmunk here at the movie?

No. As the kid burst out through the auditorium door, I could see him clearly.

JOE SWEETY!

The Big Sweety was running out of the auditorium, screaming like a two-year-old!

Whoa, dudes. I couldn't miss this.

Using all my strength, I pulled free of The Ecch. And I flew into the aisle. Running hard, I followed Joe Sweety out of the back door of the Student Centre.

Joe tore across the grass towards his dorm, screaming all the way.

"Do you believe it?" I said to myself. "The biggest, meanest, scariest dude in school is afraid of ghosts."

A grin spread across my face. I rubbed my hands together.

The answer to my prayers!

This is going to be fun, fun, fun with a capital F-U-N.

We're going to HAUNT Joe Sweety!

Chapter 11

THE NYCE HOUSE GHOST

Later I closed the door to my room. I paced back and forth for hours, planning and plotting. Then I did some plotting and planning.

Nobody can plan and plot and plot and plan like Bernie B

Finally, I had the perfect idea.

I was going to make Joe Sweety think there was a ghost in Nyce House, his dorm. And that it was after HIM!

Could I do it? Does a salmon have a nose?

I needed Feenman for the first part of my plan. I

told him exactly what to say. Then I took him to the gym.

Joe Sweety lifts weights in the gym every morning before classes. Sometimes when the gym is locked, Joe lifts Coach Bunz's car instead.

Sure enough, there was The Big Sweety, huffing and puffing in the centre of the floor. He was only lifting 100-kilo weights this morning. Guess he wanted to take it easy.

I pulled Feenman close to him. I wanted to make sure Joe heard everything we said. "He's listening," I whispered to Feenman. "Remember, repeat everything I told you."

Then I started to talk very loudly. "The Nycc House ghost is a hundred years old. He returns every five years," I said. "And he always goes after guys named Joe."

I glanced behind me. That *definitely* caught Joe's attention.

"Why only guys named Joe?" Feenman asked.

"A hundred years ago, when the ghost was a Rotten School student, a big dude named Joe used to sit on him and tickle him till he peed. Soon the poor kid died of embarrassment. And since then, he hates anyone named Joe. Every five years, he returns to Nyce House to haunt *another* Joe!"

I heard a loud thud. The floor shook. Sweety had dropped a weight on to his foot.

He hopped over to me on his other foot and grabbed me by the shoulders. "You're joking about that ghost – right? Tell me you're joking."

"Oh. Sorry," I said. "I didn't know you were listening. Don't pay any attention. Just because *everyone* is talking about it doesn't mean it's true."

"Don't worry about it," Feenman added. "The ghost only comes once every five years."

"How many years has it been?" Joe asked.

I pretended to count on my fingers. "Uh…five," I said. "But don't worry about it, Joe. The ghost only comes in months with the letter *r* in them."

Sweety went pale. "But *this* month has an *r* in it!" he cried. He grabbed the front of my shirt. "Listen, how can you tell if it's haunting *you?*"

"Don't worry about it," I said. "Do you still weigh yourself every morning to make sure you're the biggest, meanest fourth grader?"

"Yeah. Of course," Sweety replied.

"Well, then," I said, "you can tell if the ghost is after you. It uses its spirit powers to make you lose weight."

Sweety's mouth dropped open. "Huh? Lose weight?"

"That's the first sign," I said.

"Don't worry about it," Feenman said. "The ghost only goes after Joes who are left-handed."

"But… but…" Sweety sputtered. "I'M left-handed!"

"Don't even *think* about it," I said. "It's just a dumb legend. Forget we even mentioned it."

Sweety nodded. His chin was trembling. He turned and hopped out of the gym on his good foot.

Feenman and I laughed. We touched knuckles and did the secret Rotten House Handshake.

"Did you see the look on his face?" Feenman said. "He's terrified."

"Call that terrified?" I said. "Bernie B hasn't even *started* yet!"

Chapter 12

THE GHOST IN THE COMPUTER

After classes I hurried back to Rotten House. I had a lot more plotting and scheming to do.

I stashed my backpack in my room. Then I ran downstairs to see Billy the Brain.

Billy is the smartest dude at Rotten School. He's so smart, he does crossword puzzles without even looking at the clues!

Billy works hard for his C-minus grade average. He studies almost half an hour every night.

That's *awesome*, right?

I needed Billy for Part Two of my plan to haunt

Joe Sweety. I found him hunched over his desk, studying hard. He was scribbling frantically into a notebook.

"What's up, Brain?" I asked. "What are you doing?"

"I'm doing my maths problems in invisible ink," Billy said. "Just to make it a little harder."

"Cool," I said.

I told you the dude is a genius!

"We're haunting Joe Sweety," I told him. "We want to get revenge for Chipmunk."

He grinned. "Nice!"

"I have a job for you. Can you hack into Sweety's computer?" I asked.

"No prob," Billy said.

"Here's what I want," I said. "When he turns on his computer, I want him to see two huge, scary *black eyes* staring out of the screen at him."

"No prob," Billy said.

"And then Sweety hears a whisper: '*I'm coming… I'm coming for you!*'"

"No prob," Billy said. "That's too easy. I'll get it going tonight."

His smile faded. "I just have one problem with my computer, Bernie," he said.

"Problem?" I said.

"It's this foot pedal. The cord is too short. It doesn't reach the floor."

My mouth dropped open. "Foot pedal?" I cried. "Billy, that's not a foot pedal. That's the *mouse*!"

"Oh," Billy replied. "I kept trying to step on it."

I squinted hard at him. "Are you sure you can do this ghost thing?"

"No prob," Billy said. "We'll scare him to death, Bernie. I promise."

I went back up to my room with a smile on my face. But the smile didn't last long. Joe Sweety stood in the doorway to my room – and he didn't look happy.

He grabbed the front of my shirt and lifted me off the floor. "Get ready to meet Mr Fist and Mr OTHER Fist!" he boomed. "I know the truth, Bernie. There *is* no Nyce House ghost!"

Chapter 13

ALWAYS TELL THE TRUTH

"Huh?" I gasped. "Put me down, Joe. Please. You're wrinkling my skin! I *hate* wrinkled skin."

"Admit it!" Sweety roared. "There *is* no ghost. The guys at my dorm said you were just trying to scare me."

Think fast, Bernie. Think fast!

"Uh…who were you talking to?" I stammered.

"Sherman Oaks and Wes Updood and my friends at Nyce House," Sweety said. "They said they never heard of a ghost that goes after Joes. They said there's no ghost that makes people lose weight. They said you made it up."

"Well…"

Sweety lifted me higher. "Is it true you made it up?"

"Yes, it's true," I said.

He dropped me to the floor. I rubbed my sore chest. "You listen to your friends, Joe," I said. "Don't listen to me."

He narrowed his little round eyes at me. "My friends are right?"

"Yeah, sure," I said. "Don't listen to me. Your friends are all geniuses, right? I don't know anything."

He stood there, breathing hard, staring at me. I could picture his pea brain spinning in his skull. I had him totally confused now. He didn't know *what* to think.

"Forget the whole thing," I said. "Your friends are right. *No way* could it be true."

"You're lying – *aren't* you?" Sweety said. "It *is* true!"

"No, Joe. Don't believe a word I said. There *is* no ghost. Listen to your friends."

"You're lying! There *is* a ghost!" Sweety cried.

"You're lying. I can tell. There *is* a ghost – and it's after me!"

He went screaming down the stairs.

Man! This was *too easy*!

Chapter 14

SWEETY LOSES WEIGHT

The next morning I woke up, stretched and smiled at the big poster on my wall. The poster of ME smiling back at me. It always starts my day off right.

My friend Belzer brought in breakfast. Belzer brings me breakfast in bed every morning. Good kid, Belzer. But sometimes the toast is too crunchy and I have to send him back for more.

"Belzer, did you sneak into Joe Sweety's room at Nyce House?" I asked.

He nodded as he poured my orange juice.

"And did you turn his scale back?" I asked.

Belzer nodded again. "I turned Sweety's scale back three kilos. When he weighs himself, he'll think he lost three kilos."

"Turn his scale back three kilos every morning," I said. "He'll be terrified. He'll think the ghost is shrinking him."

I squinted at Belzer. "What's that T-shirt you're wearing under your blazer? Let me see it."

He opened his blazer. I read what it said on his T-shirt: DON'T BLAME ME. I WAS BORN LIKE THIS.

I shook my head sadly. "Belzer, that's a loser T-shirt," I said.

He stared at me. "Do you think so?"

After breakfast, I ran into Joe Sweety on my way to classes.

"Are you OK, dude?" I asked. "You look kinda skinny."

Joe's chin quivered. He kept blinking very fast and licking his lips. "Bernie, I… I lost three kilos!" he stammered.

I shook my head. "No way," I said. "Three kilos?

How weird is that?"

"The... the ghost..." Joe murmured.

"You still believe in that ghost thing?" I asked.

"It's after me, Bernie," Sweety said.

"No way," I said again. "No ghost would come after you, Joe. You've got nothing to worry about. Know what I heard? I heard the Nyce House ghost only haunts Joes from Toledo, Ohio. So forget the whole thing."

Sweety gasped in horror. "But... but... but..." he sputtered. "I'm from

Toledo, Ohio!"

I slapped him on the back. "Don't even *think* about it," I said. "It's a dumb legend – right?"

"Right," he said. He staggered away, muttering to himself.

"We're off to a good start," I told myself. "And just wait till tonight!"

We planned to sneak over to Nyce House. I couldn't *wait* to see the look on Joe's face when he turned on his computer – and saw the ghost staring out at him!"

Am I brilliant?

Does a bear eat salami in the woods?

Chapter 15

THE GHOST LIVES!

I couldn't think about anything else all day. I just kept picturing The Big Sweety booting up his computer and seeing the deep black eyes of the Nyce House ghost *in his* ROOM!

That night after dinner I got Feenman, Crench and Belzer together. "Sweety's room is on the first floor," I whispered. "So we can sneak over there and watch the whole thing from outside his window."

We all slapped high fives and low fives. Then we touched knuckles and did the secret Rotten House Handshake. We were *pumped*!

In a few minutes, we would be watching that big bully Joe Sweety screaming like a baby. Can life get any better than *that*?

I stuck my head out the door and peeked down the hall. No sign of Mrs Heinie. "Let's go, dudes," I whispered.

I was halfway down the stairs when I heard the scream.

A high, shrill scream of horror that sent a frozen chill down my body.

"What was THAT?" Crench cried.

"It... it sounded like Chipmunk," Belzer said.

We scrambled to Chipmunk's room.
The door stood open. We burst inside.

"Chipmunk? Chipper? Are you okay?"

I looked up and spotted him on the ceiling
again.

He clung to the ceiling light with one hand.
His other hand was trembling, pointing down to the
laptop on his desk.

"A g-g-ghost!" he stuttered. "B-Bernie! A ghost! It's after me! It's in my computer! See it?"

"Huh?" I spun around and stared at his laptop screen. "Oh, nooooo," I moaned.

Two scary black eyes stared out at me. And I heard a whispered voice from the speakers: *"I'm coming... I'm coming for you!"*

"A ghost! A ghost in my room!" Chipmunk wailed. He had his arms and legs curled around the ceiling light.

"Chipper dude, that ghost isn't looking for *you*," I told him. "It's looking for someone else. Don't worry about it."

I turned to my friends.

"Get a ladder from the basement," I said. "Bring Chipmunk down from the ceiling. Try to calm him down. Get him some vanilla pudding. That always seems to work. But make sure there are no lumps in it. He's afraid of the lumps."

Then I ran down the hall to Billy the Brain's room. I found him working a crossword puzzle blindfolded.

"What went wrong?" I cried. "What went wrong

with Sweety's computer ghost?"

He tugged off the blindfold and stared at me. "Sweety's? I thought you said I should send it to *Chipmunk*. Did I get that wrong?"

Chapter 16

TWO LEFT FEET

The next morning was cloudy and grey. I walked to classes with Belzer. He carried my backpack on top of his. Good kid, Belzer.

"Did you sneak into Sweety's room this morning?" I asked. "Did you switch school uniforms the way I told you? Did you slip him that huge uniform?"

He nodded. "Yeah, I did. No problem, Big B." He stopped walking. "Look out. Here comes Sweety now."

Sweety came stumbling up to us. His school uniform was way too big for him. The trousers dragged along the grass. The blazer kept slipping off his shoulders.

"Joe, you look different. Did you lose more weight?" I asked.

He nodded. "Bernie, do you believe it? I lost six kilos in two days!"

"You've gotta share your diet with the other guys," I said. "It's awesome! How did you do it? You eat a lot of salad?"

Sweety shook his head. "No. It's not a diet," he said. "It's the ghost. It made me lose six kilos. But I'm not worried about it."

"Huh?" My mouth dropped open. He was *supposed* to be *terrified*. "What do you mean, you're not worried?"

"I'm not worried a bit. I'm gonna trick the ghost," Sweety said.

"Trick it?"

"Yeah. I'm moving in with you."

A chill ran down my back. I couldn't breathe. I started to shake. "Move in with me?"

Sweety nodded. "The Nyce House ghost won't look for me in Rotten House. I'll be totally safe in your room."

Share a room with The Big Sweety?

Oh, no. No way. Oh, wow.

Think fast, Bernie. Think fast.

"You're right," I said. "Belzer, go help him move his stuff. Good plan. You'll be safe in my room."

Sweety stared at me. "So you agree? You think I'm right?"

I nodded. "You're totally right. Stay in my room and you'll be safe."

Joe's beady little eyes squinted harder. "You're lying, aren't you?" he said. "I can tell. You're lying again. I *won't* be safe in your room."

"Belzer, go get Joe's stuff," I said. "Bring it to my room. We'll keep Joe safe and sound. The ghost won't find him there."

"Forget it," Joe said. "I can tell you're lying! *No way* I'm moving in with you!"

He let out a sad cry. "Where will I be safe? What am I gonna do?"

I put a hand on Joe's trembling shoulder. "Calm down," I said. "The ghost isn't after you. I looked it up last night. The ghost only goes after Joes who are taller than 150 centimetres."

"But I'm 160!" Sweety screamed.

"Don't think about it," I said. "I read all about the ghost last night. You've got nothing to worry about. The ghost only goes after Joes who have two left feet!"

Sweety opened his mouth and gasped. "But... but... *I* have two left feet!" he cried. "Look!"

He frantically pulled off his shoes and socks. The guy actually has two left feet. I remembered seeing them in the gym locker room.

"Oh, wow. Maybe it *is* after you!" I said. "You haven't seen any puddles of ectoplasm in your room – have you?"

He dropped his shoes. "Huh? Ectoplasm?"

"Little green puddles," I said. "Ghosts leave puddles of ectoplasm wherever they go."

Joe stared at me in a daze. I shook him by the shoulders to snap him out of it. "Have you seen any green puddles?"

"Uh... no," he muttered. "No puddles in my room."

I slapped him on the back. "See? You're OK, dude. Nothing to worry about."

"Nothing... to... worry... about," he whispered. He staggered away on his two left feet, mumbling to himself.

Belzer and I watched him go. Then Belzer turned to me. "What's next, Big B?" he asked.

"Next we get some ectoplasm," I said. "Got any on you?"

Chapter 17

THE GHOSTLY COCOON

Feenman had a bottle of green hair gel in his room. We all agreed the hair gel would make perfect puddles of ghostly ectoplasm.

"Why do you have green hair gel?" I asked Feenman. "You don't put it on your hair."

"No way," Feenman said. "I *drink* it."

Figures.

I took the bottle from him and handed it to Belzer. "Sneak into The Big Sweety's room late tonight while he's sleeping," I said. "Drop little puddles of this all over the room."

Belzer saluted. "You got it, Big B!"

"And don't forget to set his scale back another three kilos," I said. I had a big grin on my face. Haunting Joe Sweety was *too much fun*!

The next morning, Sweety was waiting for me outside Rotten House. He was blinking and twitching and trembling.

He kept clenching and unclenching Mr Fist and Mr OTHER Fist. Sweat poured down his forehead.

Was he scared?

Does a trout swim naked?

I pretended to be worried. "Joe, are you sick or something?" I asked. "You don't look too good."

He twitched and blinked some more. "Bernie, it's after me. For real."

"No way," I said. "Stop thinking about it, Joe." I started to walk to class.

He hurried after me, stumbling in the pants that were totally too big for him. "Listen to me, Bernie. The ghost was in my room. I saw ectoplasm all over the place."

I stopped and stared at him. "How do you know it was ectoplasm?"

"It was drippy and green," Sweety said. His voice cracked. "I tasted it. It tasted like hair gel. But it was definitely ectoplasm."

"Don't worry about it," I said.

He gasped. "Don't worry about it? The puddles came right up to my *bed*!"

"Don't even think about it," I said. "I checked out more info on the Nyce House ghost."

"Yeah? What did you find out?"

"You've got nothing to worry about. It only goes after Joes with a middle name that starts with Q!"

"OH, NO!" Sweety wailed. "My middle name is Quisenberry!"

"Uh-oh," I muttered. "Well… at least he didn't wrap you in a cocoon."

Sweety gulped. "Excuse me? A cocoon?"

"Oh. Never mind," I said. "I didn't mean to say that. Just ignore it. It won't happen to you."

"Tell me," Sweety insisted. "Tell me about the cocoon."

"That's how the Nyce House ghost destroys his victims," I said. "He wraps them up tightly in a ghostly cocoon. And there's no way they can ever escape."

Sweety squinted at me. "You're lying, aren't you? There aren't any cocoons – right?"

"Yes, I'm lying," I said. "You caught me. I just made up the cocoon thing."

He squinted at me some more. "No. *Now* you're lying!" he cried. "The ghost DOES wrap its victims in a cocoon!"

"I never lie," I said. "Cross my heart."

"That means you're lying," Sweety said. "The ghost is gonna try to *cocoon* me! I know it!"

"Don't worry about it, Joe. You're totally safe," I said. "Totally. Trust me."

I watched him wobble off to class. Then I hurried to find Feenman, Crench, and Belzer.

"Meet me after dinner," I said. "We're almost finished haunting Joe Sweety. Now we've gotta get the cocoon ready."

Chapter 18

A Thousand Caterpillars

"How do you make a cocoon?" I asked Billy the Brain.

He was reading a manga comic book. He reads them in the original Japanese. And he holds them upside down to make it even *harder*!

Billy scratched his chin. "How do you make a raccoon?"

"No," I said. "A *cocoon*. A really BIG cocoon."

He nodded. "Well... *caterpillars* make cocoons. Before they become butterflies. So, Bernie, you need to collect a few thousand caterpillars."

I squinted at him. "Billy, where do I get a few thousand caterpillars?"

"Beats me," he said. "Maybe a caterpillar store?"

Sometimes I think Billy needs a new nickname. Like maybe Billy the *Moron*.

I had a better idea for the cocoon.

I dug around in my closet and found cans of white Crazy String. You know. You squeeze the top and miles of sticky string pour out.

The Crazy String was left over from Halloween. Feenman, Crench and I leaned out of our third-floor window and squirted everyone who passed by down below. It was an awesome Halloween.

The white Crazy String would make a perfect cocoon. Late that night I got my guys together. I passed out the cans of string.

"This is the big finish," I told them. "After tonight Joe Sweety will never bully another kid at Rotten School."

We cheered and slapped high fives and touched knuckles and did the secret Rotten House Handshake.

"Crench, where's your mobile phone?" I asked. "Bring it. We need to take pictures of this."

He raised his phone and clicked my picture.

"Not yet!" I cried. "Don't take *my* picture. What's the matter with you?"

"You said to take a picture," Crench said.

I clicked Crench's phone shut. "Just wait. We're gonna sneak into Sweety's room and cocoon him – right? When he wakes up, he'll leap out of bed screaming and crying like a frightened baby. *That's* when you take *his* picture."

"I get it, Bernie," Crench said. "Then we'll send it to everyone in school."

"You got that right," I said. "When everyone sees what a scaredy-cat he is, he won't be The Big Sweety anymore. He'll be The Big Who Cares!"

I slapped my buddies on the back. "OK, dudes," I said. "Grab your cans and let's go do it!"

Chapter 19

THE BEST PLAN EVER

We crept out into the hall. This was the most dangerous part of the mission. If Mrs Heinie caught us sneaking out of the dorm in the middle of the night, we were dead meat.

We slithered to the stairs, walking on tiptoe so the wooden floors wouldn't creak. We were halfway down when Feenman let out a huge, roaring burp.

The burp echoed down the silent hall.

I grabbed Feenman. "What is *wrong* with you?" I whispered. "Do you want us to get caught?"

"I can't help it, Bernie," he whispered back. "I

had a cucumber after dinner. Cucumbers make me burp."

"Why did you have a cucumber after dinner?" I asked.

He shrugged. "Why not?"

He tried to cover his mouth. Not in time. Another burp shook the banister.

We froze, listening for Mrs Heinie's footsteps.

Silence.

"I'm warning you, Feenman," I whispered. "The next time we have a top secret mission – no cucumber!"

"I can't promise," he answered. "But I'll try."

We crept out of the front door. It was a cool, windy night. The trees on the Great Lawn were bending from side to side. Clouds covered the moon.

I watched a fat squirrel scamper across the grass. It vanished into the apple trees. Now we were the only ones moving across the campus.

We made our way quickly to Nyce House, holding our Crazy String cans at our sides. Feenman and Crench started bumping each other – just for fun. Feenman burped again.

I spun round. Did someone hear it? No. No one in sight.

Bright yellow lights made the stone columns at the front entrance of Nyce House glow. We kept in the shadows and sneaked around the side of the building to the back.

Sweety's room was on the first floor near the end. The three of us stopped at his window to catch our breath.

The window was half open. I peeked inside, but I couldn't see anything in the darkness.

"He must be sound asleep," I whispered. "Remember, cover him in string. Then get ready to take his picture."

Crench slid the window up higher. One by one, we climbed into Sweety's room.

Holding my breath, I crept close to his bed. I could hear him snoring lightly. He was sleeping uncovered. Perfect!

I couldn't help it. I started to giggle.

Was this the *best* Bernie B plan *ever*?

I motioned to my two buddies. We raised our cans, pressed the tops and started to cocoon him.

"Easy. Easy," I whispered. "Spread the stuff softly."

My heart pounded. My hand shook as I let the stringy stuff pour out.

And then the lights flashed on.

I jumped. I blinked. I gasped.

"NO WAY!" I screamed. "NO WAY!!"

Chapter 20

THE LAST CHAPTER

Blinking in the bright light, I stared at the face in the bed. The face staring back at me.

"Chipmunk!" I screamed. "What are YOU doing in Sweety's bed?"

Chipmunk shook his whole body. "I… I'm covered in gook!" he cried. "I'm sticky. I'm trapped. I'm all gooky!"

"But…but…" I sputtered.

"I'm gooky! I'm ooky! I'm yucky!" Chipmunk cried. His eyes bulged. "Bernie… YOU did this? YOU were trying to scare me?"

"N-no," I stammered. "No way. I—"

I turned and saw Joe Sweety standing at the light switch. He growled. "Caught ya."

"No. Wait—" I said.

Chipmunk sat up. He pulled hunks of sticky string off his pyjamas. "I've been sleeping here in Joe's room," he said, "because Joe said he'd protect me from the ghost."

"The ghost?" I cried.

Chipmunk nodded. "Joe and I are *both* afraid of ghosts. So we teamed up to protect each other."

Sweety moved towards me, squeezing his fists. "But now we know who the ghosts REALLY are!" he growled. "And now, Bernie, it's time for *you* to have a playdate with my two friends!" He shook his big, meaty fists.

Feenman and Crench dived through the open window. I could hear their feet pounding the ground as they ran away.

Joe Sweety closed in on me, fists raised.

"Wait! I can *explain*!" I cried. "I'm sure I can think of a good explanation. After all, I'm Bernie B – right? I can *always* explain! Give me a minute to think of something!"

The Big Sweety *didn't* give me a minute. He backed me to the wall. "Have you met Mr Fist and Mr OTHER Fist?" he asked.

"No, wait, Joe!" I said. "Ha-ha. It's just a mis-understanding. Ha-ha. We'll all laugh about this tomorrow. Ha-ha. Joe, give me a break. Please! OW! Was that Mr Fist or Mr OTHER Fist?

"Ow! Ow! Ow!"

You can stop reading now. The rest of the story is kinda painful.

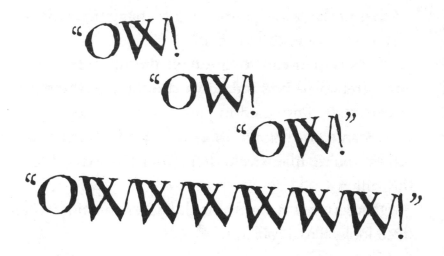

Chapter 21

ANOTHER LAST CHAPTER

Whoa. Wait. That *can't* be the end of the story.

Bernie B being pounded into hamburger meat? What kind of ending is *that*?

Let's skip ahead to the next morning. Feenman and Crench helped me down the stairs of the dorm and outside. I groaned in pain with each step.

"Bernie, you don't look too terrific," Feenman said. "You're, like, swelled up. Your head is as big as my pillow."

"Sweety has a hard punch," Crench said. "Your face looks like a *cabbage*."

"Guys, you're too nice. Stop trying to cheer me up," I said. "The swelling will go down in a week or two. And what're a few broken bones? They'll heal—right?"

Feenman shook his head. "You really look like rubbish," he said.

"No way," Crench said. "Rubbish looks a *lot* better than Bernie does!"

"*Please* stop trying to cheer me up." I groaned. "It was all worth it. I'd do it again. I did it for my friend Chipmunk. And I'd—"

I stopped because I saw Chipmunk crossing the Great Lawn, hurrying to class. "Yo – wait up!" I called.

I limped after Chipmunk. Breathing hard, I caught up to him and threw an arm around his shoulders.

"What's up, Chipper?" I said. "How's it going, dude?"

He stopped and stared at me. "Bernie? Is that you? Your face looks like a hunk of raw liver."

"You're just saying that to be nice," I said. "Listen, Chipmunk, don't thank me. Really. I did what

I did because it was the right thing to do. I don't want thanks. Please don't thank me."

He squinted hard at me. "Thank you? Why would I thank you?"

"Uh… well… for haunting Joe Sweety? For scaring him out of his head? For trying to protect you?"

Chipmunk spun around angrily. "Yeah. How could you DO that to Joe?" he screamed. "I can't believe you did that! Joe is my *friend*. You think you can pick on my friends that way?"

I took a step back. "Whoa. Chipmunk. Chill. I—"

Chipmunk raised both fists. "Come on, Bernie. I can't let you do that to my friend Joe. Come on. I'll teach you a lesson!" He swung his fists.

"OW! HEY! OWWW! STOP!"

I screamed.

Chipmunk? The shyest, most frightened kid at school – *fighting* me?

120

"OWWW!"

This really *is* the last chapter. Go away. Stop reading. I mean it. Give me a break.

"OW!
OW!
OWWW!"

Come on, beat it. Go AWAY!

HERE'S A SNEAK PEEK AT BOOK 8 IN

R.L. STINE'S

ROTTEN SCHOOL

THE TEACHER FROM HECK

Mr Skruloose glared at me. "You're ALMOST late to class."

"Almost?" I whimpered. "Almost late?"

The new teacher pointed to the floor in front of me. "Soldier, drop down and give me ten," he ordered.

"Soldier? But my name is Bernie!"

He pointed to the floor. "Drop down and give me ten."

I blinked. "Ten what?"

"Soldier, give me ten push-ups."

"I was afraid of that," I said. I turned to my friend Belzer at the next desk. "Belzer," I whispered, "drop down and give him ten push-ups for me."

"No problem," Belzer said.

Where would I be without good ol' Belzer?

The kid does everything for me. Brings me breakfast in bed... carries my backpack to class... It took weeks to put Belzer through his obedience-training. But it was worth it.

Belzer hit the floor and began straining to push his chunky body up.

"One... uh... one and a half... one and three-quarters..."

"GET UP!" Mr. Skruloose boomed at Belzer. Two of his blazer buttons popped off and flew across the room. He gave me a cold stare. "In my class, we do our own push-ups," he snarled.

I had no choice. I dropped to the floor. "It's kinda dusty down here, sir," I said. "Maybe I'd better not do this. Dust always makes me sneeze."

"SHUT UP!" he roared again. "Give me ten, soldier! Right now!"

"Could we compromise on three?" I asked.

He didn't answer in words. He just growled.

I took that for a no. I dropped down and started giving him ten.

Skruloose marched back to his desk. Some kids saluted him and he saluted back.

From down on the floor I saw Sherman Oaks jump up from his seat in the front row. His parents pay extra so he can always sit in the front row.

And they bought him a leopard-skin pillow to put on his chair so his bum doesn't get tired. I told you Sherman is a spoilt, rich brat.

Sherman walked up to Skruloose and pressed a hundred-dollar bill into his hand. "Just a welcome present from me and my friends in Nyce House," Sherman said.

Mr Skruloose crinkled up the hundred-dollar bill and shoved it into Sherman's mouth. "Are you trying to bribe me, soldier?" he boomed.

"MMMMPH-MMMMPH," Sherman replied.

"NINE... TEN!" I shouted. I climbed into my seat. Actually, I only did two push-ups – but no one was looking.

Skruloose turned to the class. He loosened his school tie. Even his Adam's apple had muscles!

"Listen up, soldiers. I'm just a farm boy," he said. "I come from Heck, Indiana. I guess you could call me The Teacher from Heck."

A few kids snickered at that. I groaned.

"But you'd better not call me that," Skruloose said. "I don't allow jokes in my classroom. And here are a few other things that I don't allow..."

He pulled out a long list and started to read:

"No glancing from side to side. No burping. No yawning. No blinking. No pencil tapping on desks. No eraser-chewing. No sneezing. Always breathe through both nostrils.

"Never come almost late to class..."

I shook my head. No lie – he really was the Teacher From Heck!

How did this HAPPEN to us?

How did we lose our old teacher, Mrs Heinie, and get the toughest teacher in the world?

ABOUT the AUTHOR

R.L. Stine graduated from Rotten School with a solid D+ average, which put him at the top of his class. He says that his favourite activities at school were Scratching Body Parts and Making Armpit Noises.

In sixth grade, R.L. won the school Athletic Award for his performance in the Wedgie Championships. Unfortunately, after the tournament, his underpants had to be surgically removed.

After graduation, R.L. became well known for writing scary book series such as *The Nightmare Room*, *Fear Street*, *Goosebumps*, and *Mostly Ghostly*, and a short story collection called *Beware!*

Today, R.L. lives in New York City, where he is busy writing stories about his school days.

For more information about R.L. Stine,
go to www.rottenschool.com
and www.rlstine.com